Louise Leblanc

Maddie Wants New Clothes

Illustrated by Marie-Louise Gay
Translated by Sarah Cummins

First Novel

Formac Publishing Company Limited
Halifax, Nova Scotia

Formac Publishing Company Limited acknowledges the support
of the Cultural Affairs Section, Nova Scotia Department of
Tourism and Culture. We acknowledge the financial support of
the Government of Canada through the Book Publishing Industry
Development Program (BPIDP) for our publishing activities.
We acknowledge the support of the Canada Council for the Arts
for our publishing program.

Canadian Cataloguing in Publication Data
Leblanc, Louise, 1942-
[Sophie prend les grands moyens. English]
Maddie wants new clothes
    (First novel series)
    Translation of: Sophie prend les grands moyens.
    ISBN 0-88780-526-4 (pbk)
    ISBN 0-88780-527-2 (bound)
I. Gay, Marie-Louise. II. Title. III. Series.

PS8573.E25S665513 2000   jC843'.54   C00-950156-8
PZ23.L393Ma 2000

Formac Publishing
Company Limited
5502 Atlantic Street
Halifax, NS B3H 1G4

Distributed in the U.S. by
Orca Book Publishers
P.O. Box 468 Custer, WA
U.S.A. 98240-0468

Distributed in the U.K. by
Roundabout Books (a division
of Roundhouse Publishing Ltd.)
31 Oakdale Glen, Harrogate,
N. Yorkshire, HG1 2JY

Printed and bound in Canada

Table of Contents

Meet all the great kids in the First Novel series!

1
Nothing to wear

I am desperate! I have searched through my closet and there is nothing! I have absolutely nothing to wear to school.

I tell you, it's like sifting through an archeological dig. Everything I own dates from antiquity.

A polka-dot sweater and a flowered shirt. To think I ever wore such things. It's incredible.

Decaying t-shirts. Blue jeans torn at the knees. Prehistoric shoes. Usually they keep antiques like these in a museum.

The rest of my stuff doesn't
fit anymore. It all makes me

look enormous, like a hot-dog bursting out of its bun.

"Maddie!" my mother calls from downstairs. "What are you doing? You'll have to leave on an empty stomach again. And—"

Good! An empty stomach is a smaller stomach!

"—you'll wind up catching a cold!'

I probably will catch a cold, since I'll have to go to school bare naked, because I have nothing to wear! Hmm ... a cold. That's it—I have a cold and I can't go to school!

As I walk downstairs, I feel myself getting sicker and sicker. I take on a dreary look and begin to sniffle. By the time I get to the kitchen, I'm half-dead.

"Still in your pyjamas!" my father scolds me. "Go back upstairs and get dressed. Now!"

"As long as she's here, she might as well eat," my mother decides. "Alexander! Give your sister a piece of your toast."

"Why do I have to?" Alexander protests. "Why doesn't Julian—"

"Because that's your fourth piece of toast and I'm only on my second," Julian retorts.

"It's not fair!" Alexander whines. "Just because Maddie sleeps late, I get less to eat."

I can't get over it! Are they all blind?

"Can't you see I'm siiick?"

"No," says Alexander.

"Really?" asks my mother, applying her hand to my forehead. She has an infallible thermometer-hand.

"No fever, not one degree!"

"But I feel so weeeak ... "

"Eat some breakfast and then we'll see."

Grrr! I sit down next to Angelbaby. She's messing around with her mashed bananas, blissfully unaware of the problems of existence.

Sometimes I envy her, I really do. Plunk! A piece of Alexander's toast lands on my plate, hard and cold. I'm about to complain when my mother announces, "We have to get some new clothes for Julian. And for Angelbaby."

That's ridiculous. "For Angelbaby? She doesn't go to school."

"So?" My father looks at me askance. "That doesn't mean she can just go bare naked."

"I need clothes more than

she does. And Julian can wear Alexander's hand-me-downs."

"At last I'll get some new clothes," Alexander crows. "I'm tired of wearing Maddie's castoffs."

"Well, I can't wear yours! It's not my fault I'm the biggest!"

"And it's not my fault I'm little," snaps Julian.

An argument flares up. It reaches fever pitch. My father cools it down with his infallible thermometer-voice.

"That's ENOUGH!"

Everyone quiets down again. "Well, Maddie," my mother remarks, "you seem to have got your energy and strength back. Go get dressed."

"I have nothing to wear!"

11

"Look in the laundry basket."

"What? You expect me to wear dirty clothes?"

"The laundry basket is full of clean clothes. You try something on, then you leave it lying around, and then you throw it in the laundry. That is taking pickiness and selfishness too far. And this applies to everyone!" she adds, looking at my father.

He chooses the easy way out, dragging me to the stairs.

"Come along! I'll find you something to wear!"

Grrr!

2
The end of my rope

My dad is so insensitive. He told me I was making a fuss about nothing, and you can't imagine what he made me wear.

The minute I stepped into the schoolyard, the nightmare began.

"Hi, Flowerpot!"

That was Sebastian, the little dandy. He always has trendy new clothes. He looks like a—

"Hi, Christmas Tree!" So there, you spoiled brat.

But it didn't make me feel

any better. Guess what my father pulled out of the laundry basket? Striped tights! With my flowered shirt, the look was—

"It's terrifying," supplied Alexander.

"It's electrifying," added Julian. "When you look at her, you get a kind of shock."

They edged away from me as if I had lice. I was all alone in the middle of an empty space. Everyone must have been looking at me.

And the worst of it was my shirt was too short. My bum showed. I hate my bum. It looks like two balloons, stretching out the stripes of my tights and making them turn pale in shame.

Yikes! There were my friends from my gang. I couldn't avoid them all day long. I might as well get it over with right away. I went over to them, hugging the side of the building.

I was ready for all kinds of

horrible comments. But no! Nobody said a word. Maybe they were in shock—an electric shock, I suppose. Their lips were squeezed tight and their eyes stared straight ahead like electric sockets.

But that didn't last long.

"Why are you wearing a Halloween costume?"

"You look like a giant doll."

"Are you disguised as Mrs. Spiegel? If you were going to make fun of the teacher, you should have told us!"

I couldn't stand it anymore. They were so mean! Worse than Sebastian. With friends like them, I certainly did not need enemies.

For a moment, I felt as if

time was standing still. I looked at each one in turn. I was so mad at them!

Nicholas, whose dad runs a corner store, always stuffing his face. But he stays as skinny as a celery stick.

Patrick, the tough guy. He's big and strong and so sure of himself. He can dress however he likes! Nobody would dare make a comment.

Clementine, Little Miss Perfect. So delicate. She can wear anything and everything looks good on her. But nobody notices her, she's such a mouse.

But everyone notices me! Especially today. I could feel tears gathering at the edge of my eyes.

"Maddie!" The little mouse sounded sorry. "We didn't mean to hurt your feelings. We were only kidding around."

I felt a slap on my back. That was Patrick's way of comforting me.

"Hey, you're not going to cry, are you, swellhead?"

"Want some chocolate?" offered Nicholas. "Chocolate is good for whatever ails you!"

I took a piece of chocolate. It went down as smooth as velvet and warmed my heart. I was with my friends!

"Do you want to tell us what's wrong?" Clementine asked.

I told them what had

happened at breakfast, only slightly exaggerating the unspeakable behaviour of my father and brothers.

My friends were appalled!

"That's what happens in large families," Nicholas remarked, tearing open a bag of chips. "But I don't see what you can do about it, unless you want to have your brothers and sister bumped off."

"That wouldn't solve my present problem," I said gloomily, helping myself to a few chips.

"Here—wear my jacket!"

For once, I was glad Patrick was so big. His jacket covered up my bum!

"You can keep it until

tomorrow. Maybe your parents will figure out that you need some new clothes."

"Not likely!" said Clementine. "Parents rarely pick up on our messages. However, there is a more persuasive method, if you are

willing to take desperate measures."

"Oh, I am!"

Never would I have dreamed that Miss Perfect could think up such a devious plan! Even I could never have thought of it.

3
Direct action

Alexander and Julian sat as far as possible from me in the schoolbus. I could hear them laughing. I thought of what Clementine had said.

"You can't have everyone in the family against you. First, you must make at least one ally."

Now was the time. The bus was stopping. My brothers got off and ran towards the house. I caught up with Alexander before he got to the door.

"I have to talk to you. It's for your own good."

He looked at me suspiciously.

"Aren't you tired of wearing my old clothes?" I asked.

"What a question! Of course I am!"

"Well, then, listen ..." And I told him the plan.

Alexander's eyes grew twice as wide.

"Are you crazy?"

"Do you want new clothes? Yes or no?"

I felt that Alexander needed to be prodded—with an electric shock.

"Don't come complaining to me when you have to wear these striped tights!"

He practically choked. I took that to mean that he agreed with my plan.

* * *

My mother greeted us absentmindedly. She was busy making a pie. It took her a minute or two to notice the jacket.

"Maddie! You know I hate you to borrow things. You must return that jacket to its owner first thing tomorrow."

My mother was obviously unaware of the desperate state of my wardrobe. How truly Clementine had spoken: our parents rarely pick up on our messages.

"I'm going to go and do my homework now," announced Alexander, giving me a conspiratorial wink.

I was about to follow when

my mother called me back.

"I would like you to feed Angelbaby. We're having guests this evening and things are a bit tight."

Grrr! I shoved a spoonful of mush into Angelbaby's mouth. Her cheeks stuffed, she cried, "MO! MO!"

In other words, more,

more! I quickly obeyed, before she started to shriek. It's amazing how much that kid can eat! I should warn her. Maybe my mother would even pick up on the message.

"You'll be enormous if you keep eating like this, Angelbaby. You won't like it. It's very bad for a girl."

"MO!"

"Okay, okay. It's very bad for a girl to have a big bum. You can't wear nice clothes. And your friends will laugh at you."

My mother didn't seem to be listening. She energetically kneaded her pie dough, raising a cloud of flour. Maybe she had flour in her ears.

"And your MOTHER will not understand the tragedy

that you—Sorry, Baby! All gone! No mo mush!"

"I'll take over now," said my mother. "I've finished here. Gran will be pleased. It's her favourite pie."

"Gran is coming?"

"Yes, she's bringing a friend to dinner. I told you."

Well, no, she hadn't told me. But it would be a waste of time to argue. I never win any argument with my mother. Besides, I had to think before I went upstairs.

Maybe Gran would be a better ally than Alexander. She is always dressed in the coolest fashions. She would sympathize with my plight, and she would be sure to buy me a present. On the other hand, she would not be able to replace my entire wardrobe.

"Pssst!" Alexander was signalling me.

I found him in the bathroom.

"I've already emptied the laundry basket," he whispered. A mountain of laundry covered the bathroom floor.

"I've got two pillowcases here, to carry the clothes downstairs. Quick, before Julian finds us!"

I had never seen Alexander so determined. The thought of the striped tights must have galvanized him.

Our sacks of laundry slung over our backs, we tiptoed downstairs. Like thieves, we stole past the kitchen door.

Then we rushed down the
basement stairs.
  "Do you remember

Clementine's instructions?" Alexander was worried.

"Wash in hot water. The hotter the water, the more the clothes will shrink."

"And the more clothes for Julian to wear!"

We both burst out laughing.

"You guys are not very nice!" It was Julian, with a sack of laundry on his shoulder. "You make plans and leave me out. But I know what you're up to."

Alexander and I looked at one another. How much did he really know, the little genius?

"You're doing the laundry to help Mom out. I want to help too. I'm going to do my laundry."

"Okay, okay!" Alexander shot me a panicked look.

"There's no time to argue," I said. "Mom might come down. Come on! We'll wash everything. Quick!"

After we emptied the three pillowcases, the washing machine was stuffed to the gills.

"You forgot the soap!" cried Julian.

"We don't need soap," said Alexander impatiently.

"You always need soap to do a wash," Julian insisted.

He picked up a huge box of detergent, stood on his tiptoes, and poured about half of it into the washing machine.

I whispered in Alexander's ear to reassure him.

"It's even better with Julian here. If anything goes wrong, he'll say that we were just trying to help out. If his clothes shrink too, that will just mean more clothes for Angelbaby."

"And Mom and Dad won't

have to buy new clothes for her! Or for Julian! Two birds with one stone. Yep. This is a brilliant plan."

4
Stop in time

DING-DONG! DING-DONG!

That must be Gran! I ran to open the door. What a terrible shock! Gran looked about thirty years older.

She usually sparkles in bright colours. Now she was wearing a dress of dull brown. Her hair was scraped back. I hardly recognized her.

She introduced her companion, Mr. Wilbur Goad. He looked as wrinkled and shrivelled as a mummy.

Alexander just gaped at Mr. Goad. Then Gran introduced

him to Julian.

"I'm very pleased to meet you, Mr. Toad," said Julian.

My parents seemed unaware of what was going on. They just acted normal. My father told us to be good. My mother asked me to look after Angelbaby.

We sat down at the dinner table right away because The Toad was used to eating early.

Gran started telling us his life story. I was so bored I thought instead about the magic transformation taking place in the basement laundry room. The washing machine was creating clothes for Julian and Angelbaby! *Abracadabra!*

I imagined myself in a store, trying on all the clothes I like. New hip-hugger jeans! I'd have to get rid of my tummy. I decided to stop eating.

"Maddie! Please come back to the table. Your grandmother has an announcement to make!"

Gran stood up and raised her glass.

"Please drink to Wilbur's health and to our marriage!"

What? Gran was getting married? To that ... fossil? The news hit me like a bomb.

POWWW!

That was the sound of an explosion! Everyone was so shocked that no one reacted, except Julian.

"It's because of taking pickiness and selfishness too far! And this applies to everyone. We did the laundry that wasn't dirty. And we didn't forget the soap and please don't get mad at us! *Sniff!*"

Under the circumstances, I thought Julian defended us very well. I had nothing to add.

My parents, however, wanted to know more. They

ran downstairs, followed by Alexander, Julian and Gran. I was left alone with Angelbaby, who was drowsing off, and with Wilbur Goad, who was already snoring. I couldn't believe it.

"Yoo-hoo!"

He didn't hear. He went on snoring. I felt like startling him awake, but I didn't do it. Then I heard the others coming back.

Do you know what had happened? There was so much laundry it absorbed all the wash water and the soap turned into a kind of paste. The motor couldn't cope with the strain and it exploded.

My mother looked as if she was about to explode too. But

she kept her cool, because she didn't want to spoil Gran's big evening.

I didn't ask whether the clothes had shrunk. When you do something stupid, it's helpful if you realize it and stop yourself in time before you make it worse!

"Aaaah!"

The Toad was finally waking up. Poor Gran. She'd die of boredom if she married him. Already she looked thirty years older. She was about to do something stupid, but she didn't realize it.

I didn't understand her at all.

5
A lesson learned

My mom came close to losing her cool the next morning when she tried to sort out the clothes.

I put on my tights without grumbling. They weren't so bad. I hadn't eaten anything since the day before, so maybe I had lost some weight. I was starving. I would get some chips from Nicholas.

I met up with all my friends in the schoolyard.

"Do you have anything to eat, Nicholas?"

"Uh ... no, nothing to offer."

"But you always have enough for the whole school!"

"I've stopped eating junk food."

"Why? Do you want to lose weight? You're so skinny you don't even need to open the door. You can just slip underneath!"

"He's not trying to lose weight," Patrick broke in. "He's off junk food because he wants to get rid of—"

"Shut up!" yelled Nicholas, turning red. "Or I'll rip off those big ears of yours!"

Patrick turned red too and jumped on Nicholas. I turned to Clementine, puzzled.

"Why are they fighting?

What is Nicholas trying to get rid of?"

"His pimples!"

"What? Those two or three tiny spots?"

"They're not tiny to him. And Patrick can't stand it if you mention his ears. He has

a complex about them."

"Patrick? I don't believe it."

"Well, of course, you wouldn't understand," the little mouse said nastily.

What had come over her? I just hoped she wasn't going to start hitting me! She knows karate. But what was she talking about?

"What do you mean?"

"You're always so sure of yourself. You're never embarrassed because everything about you is so perfect."

"What about my bum?"

"I wish my bum was like yours. My bum is as flat as two pancakes."

"Well, what do you expect, on a mouse?"

It just popped out! I thought

Clementine would be angry, but she burst out laughing. So did I. It was great.

"I guess we're all afraid that other people will find something wrong with us," Clementine reflected.

"Even my grandmother! That must be why she's changed—so her new boyfriend will like her. She's so different I hardly recognize her anymore."

I told Clementine what had happened the night before.

"So, if she gets married to that toad, she'll always be trying to please him and she'll NEVER be herself again. I have to warn her!"

"She won't listen to you. She's blinded by love. That's

why she's marrying a toad.
You should try to get him to
change his mind instead."

"He won't listen to me
either!"

"There is another method,
if you're willing to take
desperate measures."

"I'm willing to do anything
to save my grandmother!"

Clementine explained her
plan. It was even more
devious than the first one. I
was thunderstruck!

"You bag of bugs! I'll bust
you!" cried Patrick.

"I'll scalp you!" yelled
Nicholas.

"We have to stop them
before they massacre each
other," sighed Clementine.

The little mouse leapt

forward to separate the two
fighting cocks. Even if you
know karate, that takes guts.
I have to tell her how
impressive she is.

I was happy to learn that
the others think I'm all right.
And it's true—I'm not bad.
But I'd be better if I were a
little skinnier.

6
The best plan

To carry out Clementine's plan, I needed allies once again. I called my brothers into my room.

"AAAAAAH! MI AMORE-E-E-E-E!"

My parents were listening to an opera. That kind of music goes on and on, so they would leave us alone for a while. I shut the door and took the plunge.

"Gran must not get married. It would be a disaster for her."

"And for you!" exclaimed

Alexander. "You're her pet. It doesn't make any difference to us."

"We'd have a different babysitter," said Julian. "A stranger, someone mean. Who wouldn't let us watch Tintin movies three times in a row. I don't want a new babysitter, billions of blistering blue barnacles!"

"It's true we have it good with Gran," Alexander reflected. "But how can we keep her from getting married?"

"We have to cast a spell on the toad, so he'll forget about Gran and forget about getting married. A spell to make all that disappear from his mind."

"You'd have to be a magician

to do that," Alexander pointed out.

"Then we'll become magicians," I announced mysteriously.

Alexander and Julian were spellbound. Perfect!

"First we need a doll made of cloth. This one will do." I picked up Julian's Professor Calculus doll.

"Not Professor Calculus!" Julian protested. "I don't want anyone to hurt him!"

"It's just a doll, idiot," Alexander laughed.

I looked daggers at him.

"If we take off the clothes, it won't be Professor Calculus anymore, right?" So Julian took off the professor's clothes and I laid the doll on the bed.

"We must all think together as hard as we can that this doll is Wilbur Goad. I will cast a spell by sticking pins in the doll. You repeat after me: AHUM! AHUM!"

"What's that supposed to mean?" asked Alexander.

"Nothing. It's just a way of concentrating to increase our power. You have to believe! Now, be quiet. I'm about to begin."

I picked up a pin and stuck it in the doll's left ear.

"Wilbur Goad! May the memory of Gran leave your mind! AHUM! AHUM!"

"AHUM! AHUM!" my brothers repeated after me.

I did the same with the right ear. Then the doll's legs

and stomach. I put several
pins in the stomach. And last,
I stuck a pin in the doll's
head.

"Wilbur Goad! May the idea
of marriage leave your mind

forever! AHUM! AHUM!"

"AHUM! AHUM!" chanted my brothers.

The ceremony was over. But the silence hung heavy around us. Finally it was broken by Julian's anxious voice.

"He's not going to die, is he, Maddie? You didn't stick a pin in his heart, did you?"

"No. Look."

I realized then that the doll looked like a pincushion, and I figured the heart must have at least one pin it. But I tried to reassure Julian.

"We didn't wish that Wilbur Goad would die. We only wished that he would forget! You can rest easy."

I opened the door to my room.

"AAAAAHHH! LA MORTE!"

The opera was about over. Time to get in bed quickly, before our parents came upstairs.

Alexander and Julian scurried off. Whew, I was glad that was over. I was exhausted. It's very tiring ... cast ... spell ... toad.

* * *

Breakfast next morning was calm and peaceful. Probably because it was Saturday. But it felt strange, like the calm before a storm. I wasn't hungry, even though I hadn't eaten since—

DING-DONG! DING DONG!

"Who can that be?" muttered my dad.

"I'll get it!"

I ran to the vestibule, only too glad to escape from the atmosphere in the kitchen. I opened the door, and there was Gran!

"I have some bad news," she told me.

I followed her into the kitchen. She asked my mother for a cup of coffee, and then spoke very softly.

"This morning I got a call from the home where Wilbur lives. He died last night."

"I'm so-so very sorry," my father stammered.

Julian panicked totally.

"It's because of the mean babysitter. We didn't want

her! So we took Professor Calculus and we undressed Wilbur Goad. And we stuck pins in him. AHUM! AHUM! To cast a spell on him but not a death spell and please don't get mad at us. *Sniff.*"

Under the circumstances, I thought Julian defended us very well. I had nothing to add, because all of a sudden I felt ... very ... faint.

* * *

"Maddie! Are you better now?"

Gran was with me in my room. She must be really angry with me.

"You must have had quite a shock, my pet. I wanted you to know it's all right. It was very mean to wish bad things for Wilbur, but you did not kill him. He was already very ill. It was just an unfortunate coincidence."

Gran wasn't angry. I could tell her everything.

"I cast a spell on Wilbur Goad so that he would forget all about you, Gran. So you would go back to your own self. You had changed so much because of him!"

"Not really, Maddie! The way I dressed, and dinner-time, and deciding to get married—those were all Wilbur's ideas, it's true. But he knew he was dying. He was so alone. I went along with his ideas to make him happy. I believe he died a happy man."

"Oh ... that's beautiful, Gran. But I'm happy that you didn't really change. Especially since—"

I stopped. It wasn't really the right time to talk about my own problems.

"What is it, honey?"

Since she seemed interested, I told Gran about my wardrobe problems.

"And I haven't eaten anything for two days, so I would fit into my old clothes."

"That's crazy!" Gran was very cross. "That's why you fainted. And you were mad at me for changing in order to please Wilbur!"

Her tone softened.

"What you did was worse, Maddie. You would do anything to be trendy. You were willing to change not just your clothes, but your body."

"Especially my bum."

Gran thought that was very funny.

"Did you think you could shrink your bum by magic? In two days? Anyway, no one is perfect, you know. You can't make yourself sick over tiny imperfections."

"But I still want to wear the latest clothes!"

"Yes, it's fun to do that. And sometimes it seems very important, like when you're going to school on Monday morning. So I think we need to go on a shopping trip!"

"You and me, Gran? Would you buy me—but are you sure you want to go shopping today?"

"Yes, it will help me forget my sorrow. But first, you have to eat. And not chips! Come on, out of bed!"

I could have jumped for joy! Suddenly I was starving! When I think of how much time I had wasted with my crazy plans, I was disgusted with myself.

No more magic tricks.

From now on, the best plan for me is to talk it over with Gran.